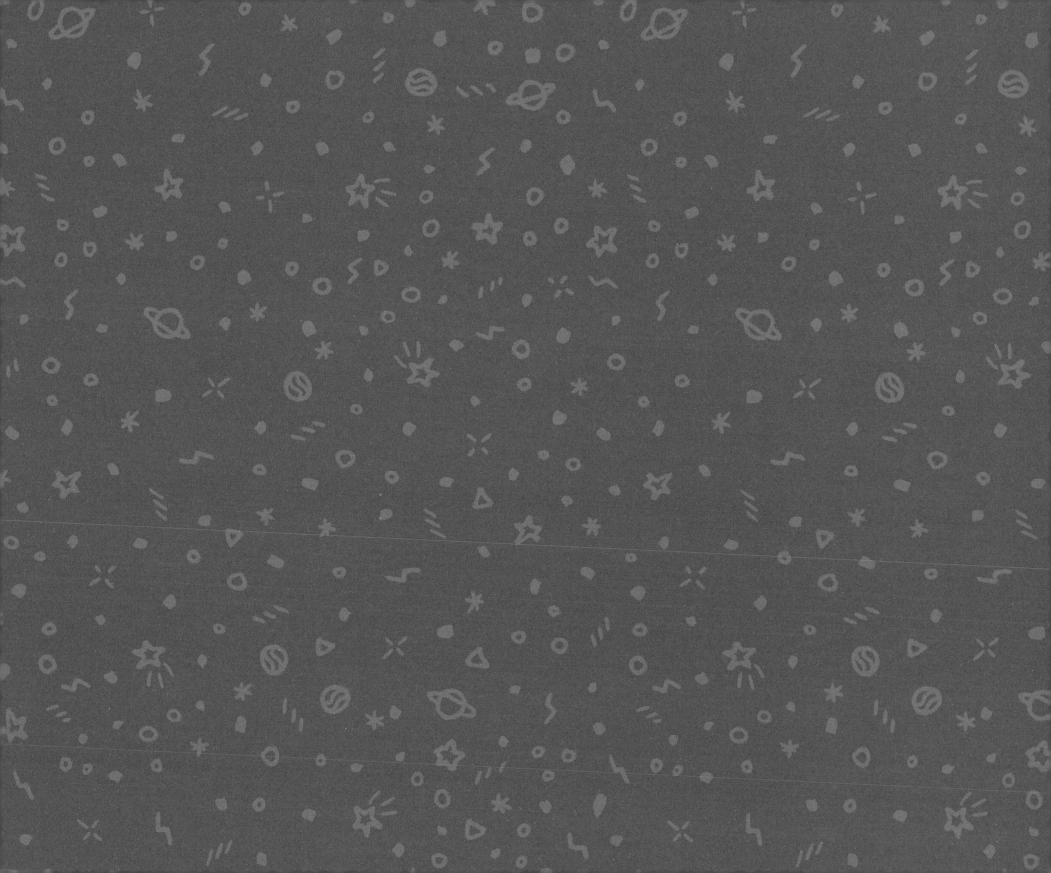

2 PIRATES +1 ROBOT

Written by Henry Herz + Illustrated by Shiho Pate

Kane Miller
A DIVISION OF EDC PUBLISHING

“What a fine haul!” said Flotsam.

“I calculate its mass at 100 kilograms,” said robot Lagan.

"Aye! I'll buy me self a bigger spaceship!" replied Captain Jetsam.

"We're rich!" cheered Flotsam. "When we return to Spaceport, I'll–"

Is Flotsam right?

BAM!
BAM!
BAM!

"Danger! Cannon blasts!" Lagan warned.

"Frigate astern!" cried Jetsam. "It's Mad Morgan – the meanest marauder of the Milky Way! He'll loot our booty!"

"We've gotta dodge those cannon blasts.
Flank speed!" Jetsam ordered.
"Left full rudder!"

"It's no use!" screamed the panicked Flotsam. "Mad Morgan's too fast! And he outguns us!"

"Steady," ordered Jetsam. "That scurvy dog ain't pilfering our plunder. Steer into that asteroid field."

"But we'll be smashed to smithereens!" yelled Flotsam.

"I calculate the odds at twenty-two percent," reported Lagan.

Did Lagan just make that up?

Twenty-two percent is better'n bein' blasted to bits fer sure if we stay!" barked Jetsam. "Hard to starboard!"

"We left 'em in our wake!" cheered Flotsam.

"Arrr. Keep yer eyes forward," Jetsam ordered. "Avoid that asteroid."

Lagan reported, "I now calculate the odds of being hit at ...

BANG!

... one hundred percent."

Did Lagan make a joke?

"Hull damage! Air pressure dropping!
What now?" yelled Flotsam.

"I will fix it," said Lagan.

A few minutes later,
a relieved Jetsam cheered,
"Well done, me lad!"

"Um, Cap'n . . .

… we're also leakin' fuel," Flotsam said.

"I calculate the leak must be sealed within ten minutes," Lagan reported. "Or we cannot reach Spaceport."

"Sink me!" said Jetsam. "We're doomed!"

"If I spacewalk, maybe I can patch the hole," offered Lagan.

"Hurry!" Jetsam cried.

“What’s takin’ Lagan so long?
We’re almost outta time!”

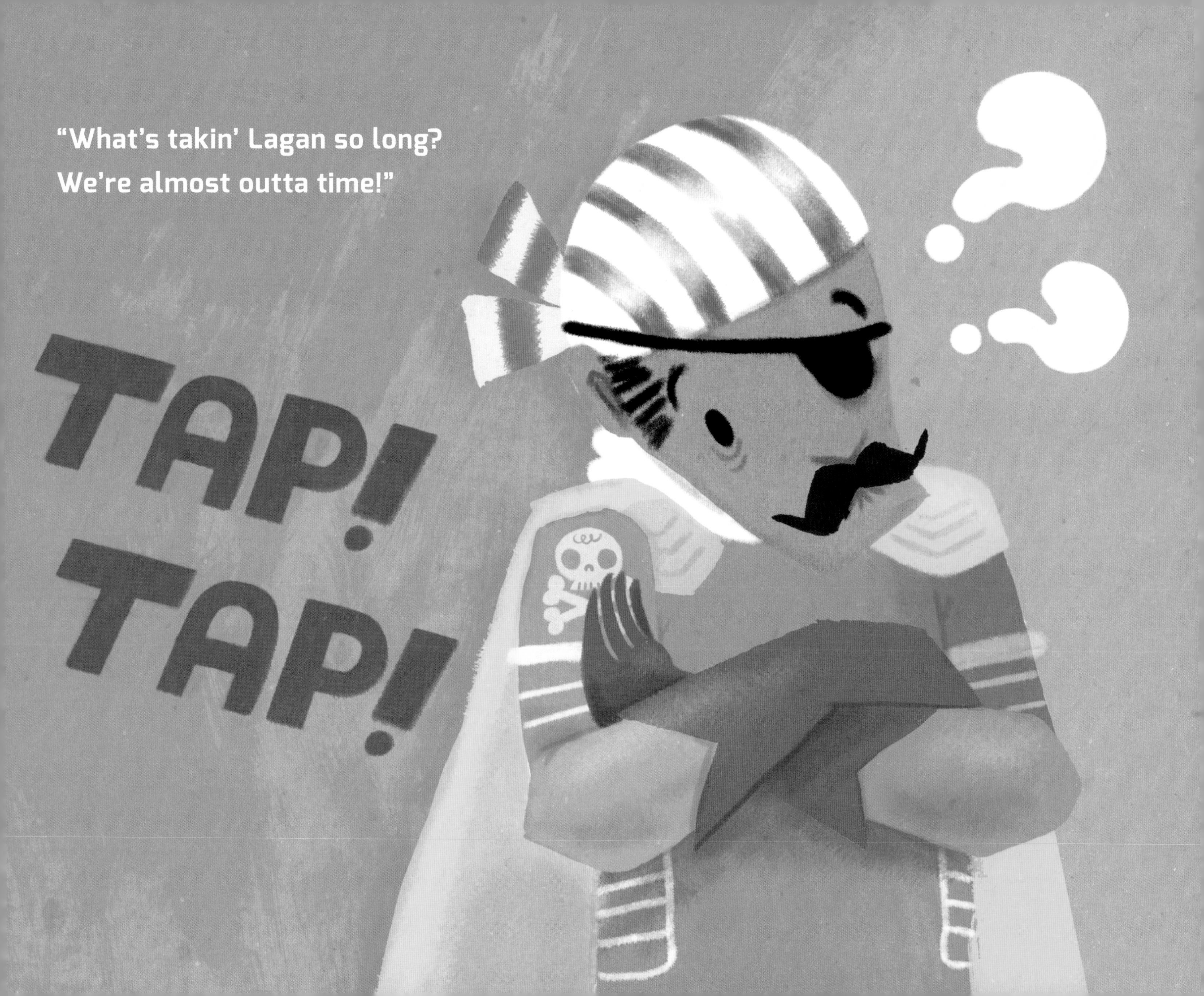

"Shiver me timbers! Yer all banged up!" exclaimed Flotsam.

"I stopped the leak," said Lagan.

"Aye," replied Jetsam, "but ...

... that took fifteen minutes. There ain't enough fuel to reach Spaceport!"

There must be something we can do, considered Lagan. He calculated. He analyzed. *That's it!* "Cap'n! A lighter ship uses less fuel."

"Clever! Start tossing things overboard, me buccos!" ordered Jetsam.

WHOOSH!

The pirates grabbed everything that wasn't bolted down.
And some things that were.

"Into the airlock with it!"

What happens
to trash
in space?

"I calculate that we must lose another ninety kilograms," reported Lagan.

"But we've nothing left to jettison!" the exhausted pirates replied.

“Cap’n,” said Lagan, “what if–”

“We’re done fer!” Jetsam sobbed, imagining being lost in space forever.

“Cap’n, I can–” said Lagan.

“I’ll never see home again!” sobbed Flotsam.

"**CAP'N!**" shouted Lagan.

"**I weigh 100 kilograms!** Jettison me!"

"Blimey, yer brave!" replied Jetsam.

"No, not that!" said Flotsam.

Jetsam sighed. "Aye. Let's do this before it gets any harder."

Lagan closed his eyes and began to shut down.

"Why did you keep me?" asked Lagan.
"The gold would have made you rich ..."

"Aye, robot. But we're richer with you as arrr friend."

Author's Note:

Robots of various types and uses exist today! They come in different shapes. Some look like people, others look like disks, insects, animals, or aircraft. Some walk, while others roll, fly, or swim. Some robots are controlled by humans, while others operate independently. They range from very big (the Global Hawk drone has a 130-foot wingspan) to the microscopic (nanorobots are small enough to travel in your bloodstream). Robots are used for many purposes, including vacuuming rooms, manufacturing (including making other robots!), keeping people company, mining, carrying heavy loads, agriculture, conducting surgery, supporting military operations, and exploring other planets.

To operate independently from humans, robots must observe their surroundings, make decisions, and solve problems. That capability is called artificial intelligence (AI). AI is a set of software rules that not only help robots figure out what to do, but also how to learn. Examples of AI include understanding human speech, playing strategy games, simulating human behavior, and driving cars.

"I calculate its mass at 100 kilograms," said robot Lagan.
How did Lagan know that?

Lagan's laser eyes scanned the gold, measuring its volume as 5,176 cubic centimeters (cm3). Since gold has a density of 19.32 grams per cm3, Lagan calculated its mass as 19.32 g/cm3 x 5,176 cm3 = 100,000 grams. There are 1,000 grams in a kilogram (kg), so the gold had a mass of 100,000 ÷ 1,000 = 100 kg (about 220 pounds).

"We're rich!" cheered Flotsam.
Is Flotsam right?

Although Flotsam isn't very good at math, he is correct in this case. The price of gold varies, but at $1,250 per ounce (oz.), 100 kilograms (220 pounds) of gold would be worth 220 lb. x 16 oz./lb. x $1,250/oz. = $4.4 million.

"I calculate the odds at twenty-two percent," reported Lagan.

Did Lagan just make that up?

No. Lagan's database indicates that the chances of being struck by any single asteroid are one in a thousand, or 0.001. That's the same as saying the chance of a single asteroid NOT hitting the ship is 1 − 0.001 = 0.999. But he counted 250 asteroids near their spaceship. Assuming the asteroids move independently from one another, Lagan calculated the chance of not being struck by ANY asteroids by raising 0.999 to the 250th power, which is 0.78. So, the chance of being struck by one or more asteroids is 1 − 0.78 = 0.22.

. . . one hundred percent."

Did Lagan make a joke?

Yes, because if something has already occurred, then the chance of it happening is 100 percent certain.

"I calculate the leak must be sealed within ten minutes," Lagan reported.

Why must the leak be fixed so quickly?

The ship's control panel shows 5,000 liters of fuel left, and that they'll need 4,000 liters to reach Spaceport. So, they can afford to lose no more than 5,000 − 4,000 = 1,000 liters. The control panel also indicates that they're leaking fuel at 100 liters per minute. Lagan calculates that the spare fuel will be gone after 1,000 liters ÷ 100 liters/min. = 10 minutes.

WHOOSH!

What happens to trash in space?

Normally anything in space (including trash) moves with whatever inertia is imparted to it. So, if you threw a baseball in space at 30 mph, it would keep moving at 30 mph until another force was applied to it, like gravity or bumping into something. There is trash from space launches orbiting the Earth today. However, in our story, since the ship is passing very near an uninhabited planet, the trash will be drawn in by gravity, and burn up from the friction of falling through the planet's atmosphere.

"I calculate that we must lose another ninety kilograms," reported Lagan.

Why do they need to lose more mass?

When Lagan took 15 minutes to repair the leak, the ship lost 15 min. x 100 liters/min. = 1,500 liters of fuel. That left the ship with 5,000 − 1,500 = 3,500 liters. The ship's navigation computer shows that they need to reduce the ship's mass by 500 kg in order to reach Spaceport with the reduced fuel. Lagan has measured the mass of the items jettisoned so far at 410 kg. So, he calculates they need to jettison a further 500 − 410 = 90 kg.

With thanks to my wife, Bill Nye, Joss Whedon, and the Author of all things. — H.H.

To Deborah, Ryan and my Space girl Olivia. — S.P.

First Edition 2019
Kane Miller, A Division of EDC Publishing

Text copyright © Henry Herz, 2019
Illustrations copyright © Shiho Pate, 2019

For information contact:
Kane Miller, A Division of EDC Publishing
www.kanemiller.com
www.edcpub.com
www.usbornebooksandmore.com

Library of Congress Control Number: 2018958195

Manufactured by Regent Publishing Services, Hong Kong
Printed August 2019 in Shenzhen, Guangdong, China
1 2 3 4 5 6 7 8 9 10

ISBN: 978-1-61067-812-4

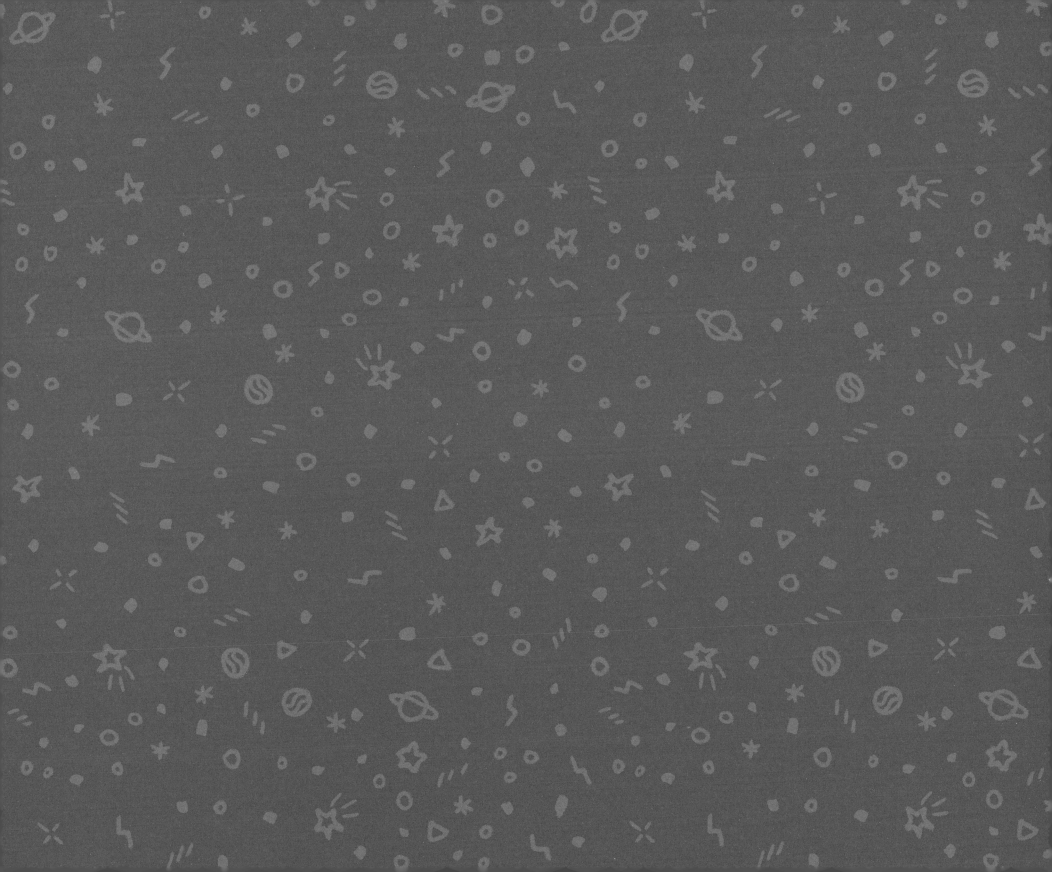

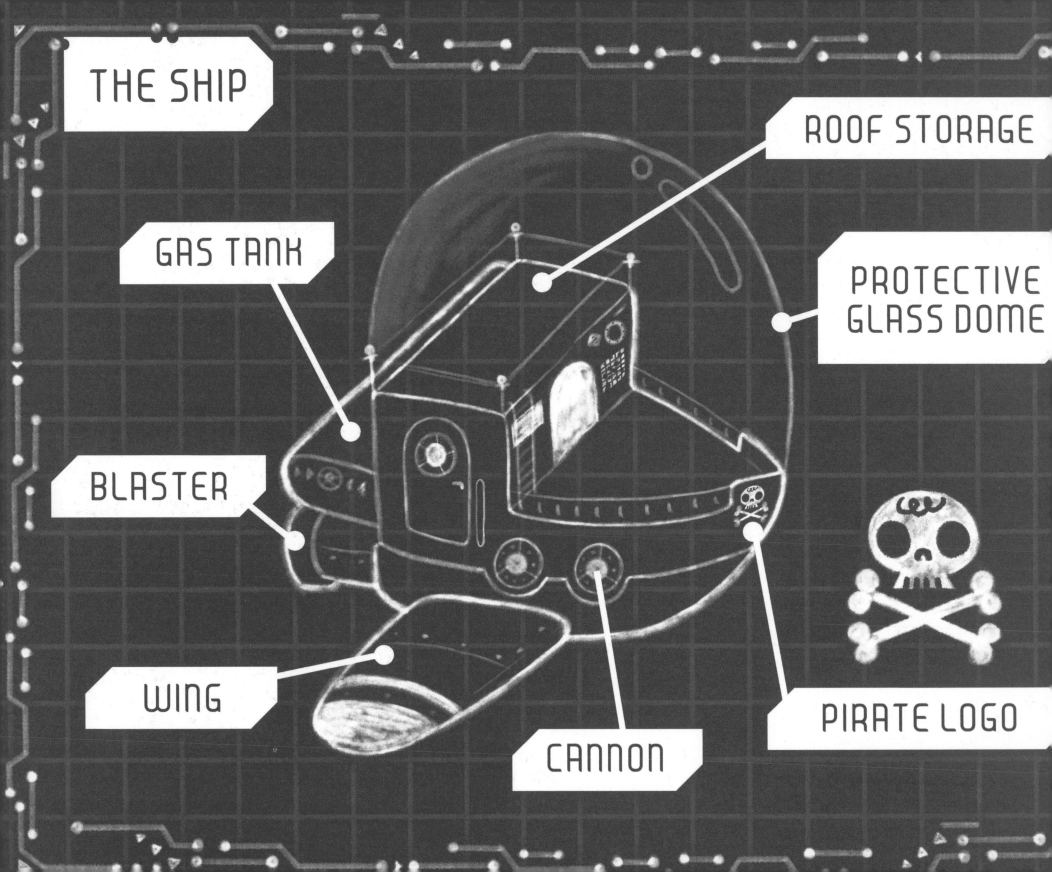

THE SHIP

ROOF STORAGE

GAS TANK

PROTECTIVE GLASS DOME

BLASTER

WING

CANNON

PIRATE LOGO